Mama and Daddy Bear's Divorce

Cornelia Maude Spelman

ILLUSTRATED BY Kathy Parkinson

Albert Whitman & Company
Morton Grove, Illinois

For all the little bears. —C. M. S.

For Trevor and Abby, with love and my very best wishes. —K. P.

Library of Congress Cataloging-in-Publication Data
Spelman, Cornelia Maude.
Mama and Daddy Bear's divorce / by Cornelia Maude Spelman; illustrated by Kathy Parkinson.
p. cm.
Summary: Dinah Bear feels sad and scared when her parents say they are going to divorce.
ISBN: 978-0-8075-5221-6 (hardcover)
ISBN: 978-0-8075-5222-3 (paperback)
(1. Divorce—Fiction. 2. Bears—Fiction) I. Parkinson, Kathy, ill. II. Title
PZ7.S74727Mam 1998
[E]—dc21 98-9299
CIP
AC

The art is rendered in colored pencil and watercolors.
The design is by Scott Piehl.

For more information about Albert Whitman & Company,
please visit our web site at www.albertwhitman.com.

Note to Grownups

To the very young child, divorce need be explained only in the simplest terms. The child will mostly be worried that he or she will lose the parent who lives elsewhere—usually the father. So a child needs to be reassured that this won't happen.

Young children are comforted by sameness, as any parent who's tried to change a single word of a child's favorite story knows well. This book emphasizes the precious things in a child's life that stay the same.

As children grow they can understand more complex reasons for the divorce, but to the very young child, divorce simply means that he or she no longer has both parents in one place. *Mama and Daddy Bear's Divorce* conveys the message that no matter where the parents live, they will always love their child and be a part of his or her life.

—Cornelia Maude Spelman, A.C.S.W., L.C.S.W.

Dinah had three favorite people—her mama, her daddy, and her big sister, Ruth.

She had two favorite things—Bunny, her stuffed rabbit
with one ear, and her red sandals with the three straps.

Dinah liked making bread with Mama and Ruth.

She liked taking walks with Daddy and Ruth.

She liked going to sleep with Bunny's ear next to her cheek,

and she liked putting on her red sandals with the three straps.

But one day something sad happened. Mama and Daddy said they were going to get a divorce.

A divorce meant that Daddy would not live with Mama, Ruth, and Dinah anymore.

Dinah felt sad and scared. She didn't want Daddy to go away. Where would he go? Would she see him again?

Daddy touched her gently and said, "You will come visit my new home every weekend. Even if I don't live with you, I will always be your daddy."

"Ruth's, too?" asked Dinah.

"Ruth's, too," Daddy said.

After Daddy moved to his new home, Dinah still made bread with Mama and Ruth. At night she still went to sleep with Bunny's ear next to her cheek. Every morning she still put on her red sandals with the three straps.

But she missed Daddy very much.

When Dinah and Ruth went to stay at Daddy's new home, Dinah still took walks with Daddy and Ruth. She still slept with Bunny's ear next to her cheek. In the morning she still put on her red sandals with the three straps.

But she missed Mama very much.

Dinah wished she could have Mama, Daddy, Ruth, and her favorite things all in the same place. Sometimes she cried. Then Mama or Daddy would hug her.

"I will always be your daddy," said Daddy.

"I will always be your mama," said Mama.

Dinah and Ruth stayed with Mama during the week. On Saturdays Daddy came to pick them up. Dinah was happy to see his face smiling at her.

And on Sundays she was happy to feel Mama's arms around her again.

When it was Dinah's birthday, Daddy came for cake.

Then Dinah had a second party at his home.

Sometimes on Saturdays Daddy was busy, and Dinah and Ruth didn't visit. One time he couldn't pick them up when he said. Then Dinah squeezed Bunny very hard.

But even when she couldn't
see Daddy, they could talk
on the phone

and send letters to each other.

As time went by, Dinah was not so sad. Even if there had been a divorce, Ruth would always be her sister, her daddy would always be her daddy,

and her mama would always be her mama.

And they all loved her very much.